a gift for:

from:

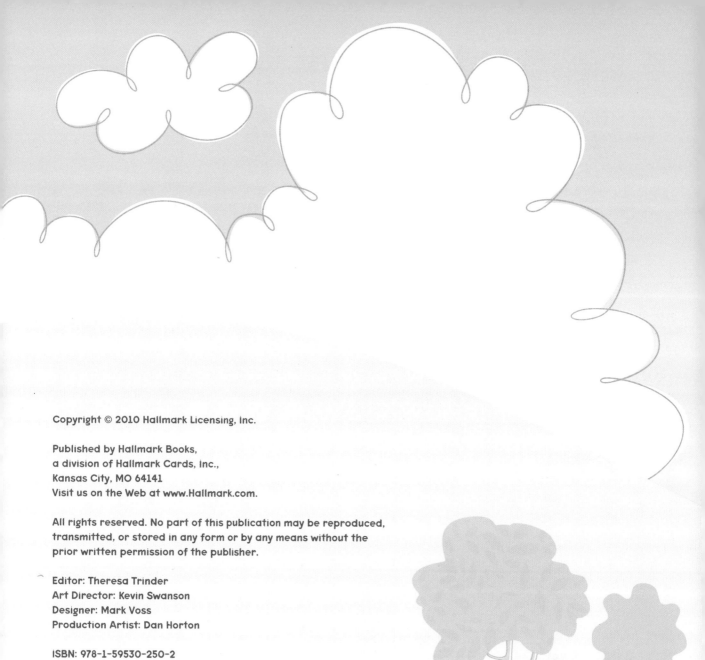

Published by Hallmark Books,
a division of Hallmark Cards, Inc.,
Kansas City, MO 64141
Visit us on the Web at www.Hallmark.com.

Editor: Theresa Trinder
Art Director: Kevin Swanson
Designer: Mark Voss
Production Artist: Dan Horton

ISBN: 978-1-59530-250-2

BOK6151

Printed and bound in China

NOV09

TiNY
tweet

By Keely Chace Illustrated by Chris Corchiani

GIFT BOOKS
from Hallmark

Tweet wasn't just little.

He was itty-bitty.
Eensy-weensy.
Teeny-beany.

Even for a baby chick, he was tiny.

It wasn't always easy
being the smallest chick
in the coop.

Sometimes he had
an even tougher time
being seen.

Every now and then,
Tweet wished he weren't so tiny.

"But you are just the right size," said Mama Hen.

"Just right for what?"
Tweet wondered.

Just right for sniffing
the buttercups?

Just right for bunny rides?

Just right for the tippy-top
of a peeping pyramid?

Or maybe just right for making friends?

"Hmm,"
thought Tiny Tweet,
"maybe Mama is right."

And when he crawled into
the coziest spot in the coop
(that only he could fit in),
he knew it for sure . . .

Tiny was just the
right size to be.

Did you enjoy this tiny little story?
We would love to hear from you.

Hallmark Book Feedback
P.O. Box 419034
Mail Drop 215
Kansas City, MO 64141

booknotes@hallmark.com